Gracie's Night

A HANUKKAH STORY

*When we are brave enough
to reach out instead of looking away,
miracles can happen.*

For David, who gave me the world.
And for Tara, Brooke & Brett, who are my world.

LYNN TAYLOR GORDON is a writer, yoga teacher, and animal lover who happily lives in southern New Jersey with her family. Celebrating Gracie's Night is a Gordon family tradition at Hanukkah. Lynn hopes Gracie's story will inspire you to start your own tradition.

LAURA BROWN is an illustrator who lives and works in Austin, Texas.

Gracie's Night would not have been possible without the insight, wisdom, and expertise of Simone Kaplan, story editor at Picture Book People; Stephanie Bart-Horvath, creative director of s.b.art.design; Janet Frick, line editor and copy editor; and Rachelle Stern, senior counsel and in-house historian for Macy's, Inc.

To contact the author, learn more about the family tradition that inspired this book, order copies, or obtain permission to quote from it, please visit graciesnight.com

Cookie & Nudge Books
cookieandnudgebooks.com

Gracie's Night
Copyright © 2013 by Lynn Taylor Gordon
Printed in Canada
Library of Congress Control Number: 2013914245   ISBN 978-0-9857353-0-2
First Edition

Gracie's Night

A HANUKKAH STORY

by Lynn Taylor Gordon

illustrated by Laura Brown

ONE LATE-AUTUMN EVENING, snow fell like lace
on the tip of the nose of a girl named Grace.

It was holiday time in New York, Gracie's city,
where light, fluffy snow had made everything pretty.

Gracie's breath swirled as she swished down the street,
with patches of snow crunching under her feet.
Tasting the snowflakes that fell from the sky,
she happily nodded as people passed by.

Store mannequins modeled their holiday best,
long shimmering dresses and handsome wool vests.
So lovely and stylish, each seemed to say,
You can be just like us if you shop here today!

But Gracie just sighed, leaning in toward the glass,
traced a heart with her finger, and hurried on past.

For right down the street and around the next block
was her favorite store, The Second Chance Shop.
It sold gently worn clothing, like sweaters and hats,
plus books, toys, and puzzles—neat stuff like that.

After *whoosh*ing inside on a cold gust of wind,
she beelined it straight to the used-mittens bin.
Her old mittens were ragged and let in the air,
so Papa had sent her to buy a new pair.

She tried on a right with
a sweet, furry cuff,

then modeled a left with
some sparkly stuff.

She doubted she'd find any twins in the batch,
but suddenly, "Ha! Two great mittens that match!"
They were just Gracie's size, in soft royal blue—
her favorite shade, and her papa's, too.

At the counter the lady asked, "Box, dear, or bag?"
"I'll wear them right now. Could you please snip the tag?"
"Of course. My big sale's on, so luck's come your way:
I'll throw in this scarf for your best friend today."
"Why, thank you!" said Gracie. "Now we'd better go—
it's time to get home." So they left in the snow.

On the frosty walk home they kept up a quick pace
and she held the warm mittens up close to her face.
They expertly leaped over puddles and ice,
then met a French poodle who was *oh là là* nice.

When Gracie found Papa asleep in his chair,
she gave him a hug so he'd know she was there.
"Thank you, my papa!" she playfully said
as she swirled her new mitttens on top of his head.

PAST DUE

She showed him the mittens. "So what do you think?"
"Now your hands will be warm," he replied with a wink.

They shared their apartment with Gracie's dog, Max, a loyal, old boy who did tricks for his snacks.

A goldfish named Lox and a stray cat named Bagel each had a place at their small kitchen table.

They played cards and checkers and had lots of fun,
but money for extras? There simply was none.

No dance lessons, restaurants, or fancy new clothes,
just bargains and hand-me-downs. Plenty of those.

A *ping* in a pail meant the ceiling was leaking;
the old heater *ding*ed and the floorboards were creaking.
Although there were holes in his old thinking chair,
that didn't stop Papa from thinking things there.

He worked as a bus driver during the day
on a crosstown route for the MTA.
Though he worked very hard, and worked overtime too,
he still couldn't pay all the bills that were due.

With Hanukkah coming and little to spend,
Gracie declared, "All this worry must end!"

On Thanksgiving morning the BIG paper came.
Gracie studied the want ads, and one had *her* name!
HOLIDAY HELP, in big letters it read.
She circled it twice.
"That's for me!" Gracie said.

Now Gracie was Employee 488
at Macy and Company. Isn't that great?

Because she was short, at first some things were rough,
but she soon found a way to become tall enough.
And Gracie liked math, so she made change with ease
and always remembered a *Thank you* and *Please.*

She sold neckties and perfume and chocolate candy.
The shoppers loved Gracie. Her job was just dandy!
Eight presents for Papa, eight Hanukkah nights,
and money to shop with—what a delight!

With pencil in hand Gracie shopped every floor
and checked off each gift as she moved through the store.
She bought mittens and sweaters, snow boots and socks,
and had them gift-wrapped with a bow on each box.

When her shopping for Papa was finally complete,
Gracie felt happy and light on her feet.
She glided across Macy's smooth marble floor
and, twirling her bags, stepped out of the store.

It was snowing outside, a bitter-cold night,
when Gracie beheld . . .

. . . the saddest of sights:
a homeless man huddling inside a big box,
with holes in his shoes and holes in his socks.
His hands were in fists, frozen and torn.
His coat was too thin to keep this man warm.

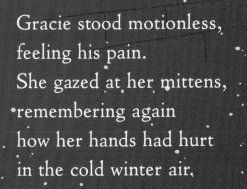

Gracie stood motionless,
feeling his pain.
She gazed at her mittens,
remembering again
how her hands had hurt
in the cold winter air.

Watching him shiver
was too hard to bear.

She left him the gifts; her decision was clear.
The man in the box never knew she was there.

She thought of her papa as she turned away.
"You did the right thing," she knew he would say.

There weren't many gifts on those Hanukkah nights.
But with Hanukkah gelt and other delights,
like crisp golden latkes and dreidels to spin,
as they lit the menorah, they felt warmth deep within.
They recited the blessings and gathered around
the glow of the candles dwindling down.

Then Gracie took Papa's gift down from a shelf:
an old wooden frame she had fixed up herself.
Now sanded and painted, the frame looked brand-new.
Her papa exclaimed, "I know *just* what to do!"

"My Gracie," said Papa, "where do I start?
I love that you have such a beautiful heart.
That man who was homeless—*he* needed warm clothes,
but I wouldn't trade you for a million of those.
You gave him a miracle, though he'll never know
it was you who stood by him that night in the snow."

"I love you, my papa," Grace quietly said.
He held her face softly, and then kissed her head.

Become someone's miracle; be someone's light!
Give up just one gift on one Hanukkah night.
Someone in need could be waiting for you.
Gracie would say, "It's the right thing to do!"